D0341325

A Midsummer Night #nofilter

For Kristina (KPT) 😘, who always makes me laugh 😜 😂 even when life gets crazy 🌀🌀 ❤️

 Published in the United States by Random House Children's Books, a division of Penguin Random House LLC, New York.
Random House and the colophon are registered trademarks of Penguin Random House LLC.

Visit us on the Web! randomhouseteens.com

Educators and librarians, for a variety of teaching tools, visit us at RHTeachersLibrarians.com

Library of Congress Cataloging-in-Publication Data is available upon request.
ISBN 978-0-553-53882-3 (trade) — ISBN 978-0-553-53883-0 (ebook)

MANUFACTURED IN CHINA
10 9 8 7 6 5 4 3 2 1
First Edition

Random House Children's Books supports the First Amendment and celebrates the right to read.

A Midsummer Night #nofilter

William Shakespeare
+
Brett Wright

Random House New York

who's who

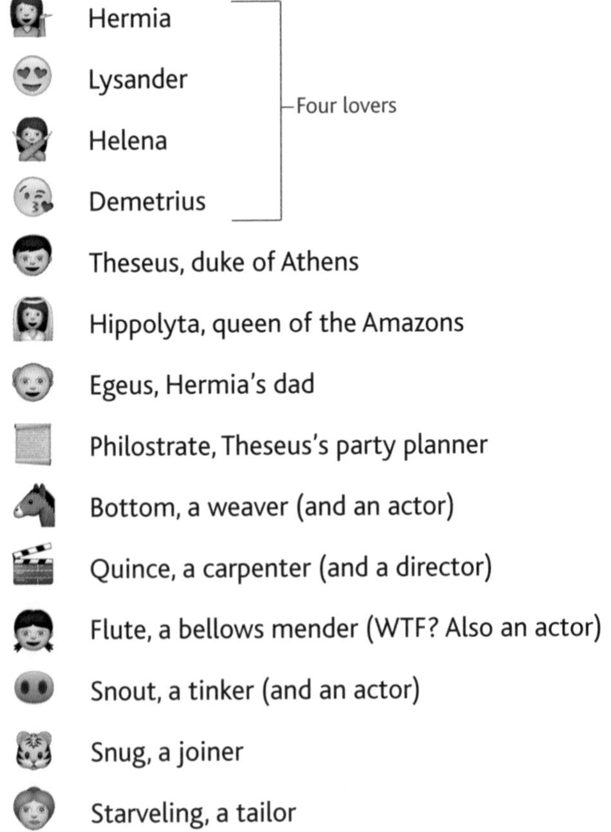

- Hermia
- Lysander
- Helena
- Demetrius

(Four lovers)

- Theseus, duke of Athens
- Hippolyta, queen of the Amazons
- Egeus, Hermia's dad
- Philostrate, Theseus's party planner
- Bottom, a weaver (and an actor)
- Quince, a carpenter (and a director)
- Flute, a bellows mender (WTF? Also an actor)
- Snout, a tinker (and an actor)
- Snug, a joiner
- Starveling, a tailor

Send

 Oberon, king of the fairies

 Titania, queen of the fairies

 Puck, a mischievous sprite

 Peaseblossom

 Cobweb

 Mote

 Mustardseed

(Peaseblossom, Cobweb, Mote, Mustardseed) — Titania's fairy servants

Send

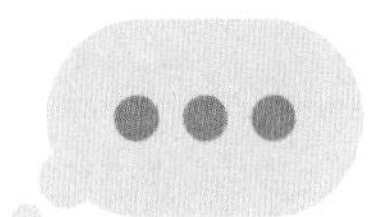

Act 1

Send

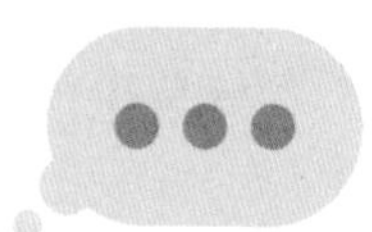

[Scene 1]

Theseus

OMG, I can't wait to get married! 

Four more days! 17 I'm not sure I can last that long.

Hippolyta

me neith! 4 more sleeps. it'll be here before u know it.

Theseus

I have a special for you: I've hired actors to put on a play in our honor.

Hippolyta

rly?? o, babe. u r 2 good 2 me! 

g2g. i've used up like 50% of my data this month, ugh. h8 payin' those fees!

Theseus

No prob, qt. It's going to be THE party of the year. 

Send

Group text: Egeus, Theseus, Hermia

Egeus

Good day, Theseus. Can you see this? 

Theseus

Hey, pal. I can see this. Why the  ?

Egeus

I don't know. My daughter, Hermia, downloaded this app onto my . I'm still learning!

Theseus

Ha! So, what's up?

Egeus

I am so ! It's Hermia, actually.

Demetrius has my permission to marry her.
But apparently she's in love with Lysander.

It's ridiculous! This isn't how her future is supposed to be.

I'm in quite a .

Send

Theseus

Think you mean pickle. That's a cactus.

Egeus

I told you, I don't know what I'm doing! 

Anyway, can I exercise my right as her father and make her obey me? Either she listens to me and marries Demetrius . . . or I have her killed, tbh.

Hermia

DAD! You know you started a group chat, right?

I can see everything you're writing. INCLUDING KILLING ME.

Egeus

Oops. I told you I wasn't ready for this kind of !

Send

Theseus

Is this true, Hermia? You know the rules. Listen to your . Demetrius is a good man.

Hermia

So is Lys! Dad just won't take the to get to know him.

Theseus

Sure. But you have to what your father is saying. ~Fathers know best.~ There's a whole day dedicated to them in June, ya know.

Let Demetrius put a on it, won't cha?

Hermia

Ugh, but no one things the way I them.

What's the worst thing that will happen if I don't marry Dem?

Send

Theseus

You'll either be put to death, or you'll have to become a nun. Sorry not sorry.

Hermia

FINE. I'd rather waste away than marry someone I'm not into.

Theseus

Why don't you take some more to think about this?

Tell ya what, four days from now—eee, btw when I get married!—I'll give you three choices: 1) you marry Demetrius, 2) you become a nun, or 3) ya die.

Hermia

These choices suck! 

Why are you so quick to agree with my without even considering my feelings?

Send

Theseus

Hmm. You make a good point. 😛 I need to know what Demetrius and Lysander have to say about all this. Let's get them in on this group chat. Will you text them, Egeus? If you can figure it out, that is. 😉

Egeus has invited Demetrius and Lysander into the group message.

Egeus

Demetrius?

Demetrius

Egeus! To what do I owe this pleasure?

Egeus

I GOT THE HANG OF IT! 👻

Kind of.

Anyway . . . Demetrius! My main man. 👍 Tell Theseus what you told me about Hermia.

Demetrius

Well, to make a long story short . . . I want to marry my sweetie! 😉

Send

And I want Lysander to Back. The Eff. Off. 

Lysander

Dude. NMF. If you and her father each other so much, why don't YOU two get married?

Theseus, I'm just as good as Demetrius. And Hermia actually wants me, which should count for something. 

Egeus

I don't know about that.

Lysander

Demetrius isn't as innocent or good as you think he is. He's no .

Did you know that he made that poor girl Helena fall in love with him? Yep. That innocent girl is head over for him even though he wants nothing to do with her!

Demetrius

Oh, PLEASE.

Send

Demetrius

That is 🐴💩 and you know it.

Theseus

Actually, Demetrius, I had heard rumors of that. Thx for confirming, Lysander. 😐 I think we need to chat offline.

Hermia

HA! 😋

Theseus

But I'm sorry, Hermia. We have to go by the law. Either you marry Demetrius . . . or get thee to a nunnery. ⛪

LOL! Sorry. Heard that in a play recently and have wanted to say it ever since. 😉

You have four days to decide. TTYL!

Send

Lysander

What's wrong, boo? I'm so sorry about that whole thing.

Hermia

This whole situation blows.

Lysander

I know. But lots of have to put up with before they can get married.

Sometimes they come from different backgrounds.

Hermia

Right. A "she's too rich and he's too poor" kind of love story. Got it.

Lysander

Or age is the problem. 

Hermia

Yes, she's barely 14 and he's pushing 40. Like that would happen. ::eye roll::

Send

Lysander

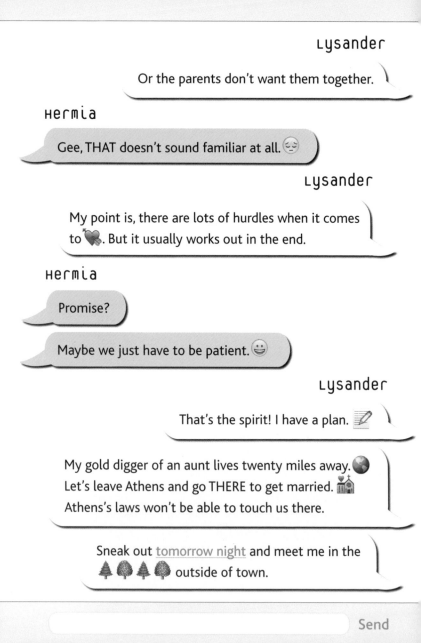

Or the parents don't want them together.

Hermia

Gee, THAT doesn't sound familiar at all.

My point is, there are lots of hurdles when it comes to . But it usually works out in the end.

Hermia

Promise?

Maybe we just have to be patient.

That's the spirit! I have a plan. 

My gold digger of an aunt lives twenty miles away. Let's leave Athens and go THERE to get married. Athens's laws won't be able to touch us there.

Sneak out tomorrow night and meet me in the  outside of town.

Send

Hermia

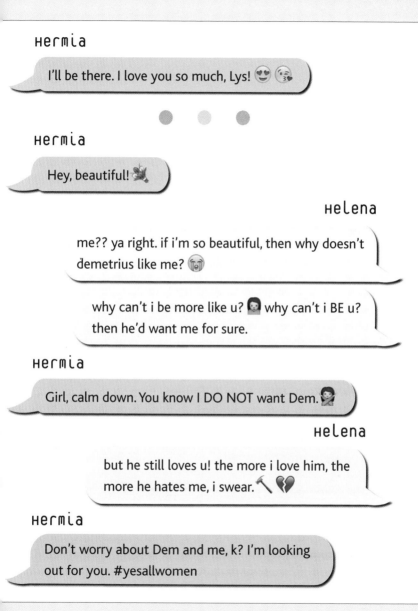

I'll be there. I love you so much, Lys!  

Hermia

Hey, beautiful!

Helena

me?? ya right. if i'm so beautiful, then why doesn't demetrius like me?

why can't i be more like u? why can't i BE u? then he'd want me for sure.

Hermia

Girl, calm down. You know I DO NOT want Dem. 

Helena

but he still loves u! the more i love him, the more he hates me, i swear.

Hermia

Don't worry about Dem and me, k? I'm looking out for you. #yesallwomen

Send

Hermia

I texted you because I'm running away with Lys tomorrow. 🏃

I can't stay in Athens anymore. Pray for Lys and me! 🙏 And I'll pray that Dem finally realizes he loves you as much as you love him! 💡 ❤️

 Helena

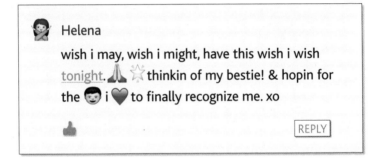

wish i may, wish i might, have this wish i wish tonight. 🙏 🌟 thinkin of my bestie! & hopin for the  i ❤️ to finally recognize me. xo

👍 REPLY

[Scene 2]

Group text: Quince, Bottom, Flute, Starveling, Snout, Snug

Quince

Hi, everyone! 👋 I'm so pumped 💪 to talk to you guys today about an exciting opportunity! You're the best actors I know in all of Athens, which means I need you to be in the play 🎭 we're going to put on for Theseus and Hippolyta's wedding! It's gonna be perfect.

Send

Bottom

Bottom here, reporting for duty!

I heard about their wedding, but I had no idea we'd get to be part of it. Cool. 😎 Tell us about the play. Who's going to get some starring roles? 😉

Quince

It's called "A Very Tragic Comedy About the Horrible Deaths of Pyramus and Thisbe."

Isn't that delightful⁉ 😀

Bottom

Hilarious! I'm dying of laughter. 😐 Now, srsly, the roles?

Quince

Since you're so eager, Bottom, you'll be playing the ⭐, Pyramus.

Bottom

Who dat? Is he an 👼 or a 😈?

Send

Quince

He's a good guy.

Who kills himself for love. 

Bottom

Ooh, drama. Guess I'll haftahave to break out the waterworks.

NP. I'll make that audience feel every I shed.

Quince

Flute, you'll be Thisbe.

Flute

OMG, yesss. The other person in the play's title! Guess I'm a too.

Who is he?

Quince

Thisbe is the Pyramus loves.

Flute

I'm playing a WOMAN??

Send

But I've been growing a BEARD! 
#practicingformovember

quince

It's fiiine. You'll wear a mask and you'll raise your voice as high  as you can. So glad you're on board!

Starveling, you'll be Thisbe's mother. 

starveling

Aw, I birthed you, Flute. 

flute

quince

Snout, you'll be Pyramus's father.

snout

LOL. K.

quince

And, Snug, you'll be the lion! 

Send

snug

 That's a tiger.

quince

Same difference!

And that's the whole cast! ☑ It's going to be marvelous.

snug

Do you have my lines ready? I need to start memorizing! 😸

quince

Ooh. About that. You don't have any lines, just sound effects. Lots of roaring. You can improvise! 👍

bottom

Let me play the lion! Grrr. 😼 In fact, I'll play ALL the parts—even Thisbe!

quince

Nope. You're the only one handsome enough to play Pyramus.

bottom

Send

snug

🙀

snout

🔫

starveling

😡

flute

🙎

quince

Terrific! So happy we're all on the same page. 📖

I'll email your scripts. Please memorize your lines by tomorrow night. Meet me in the 🌲🌳🌲🌳 and we'll rehearse. Be there or be ⬛, LOL. JK!

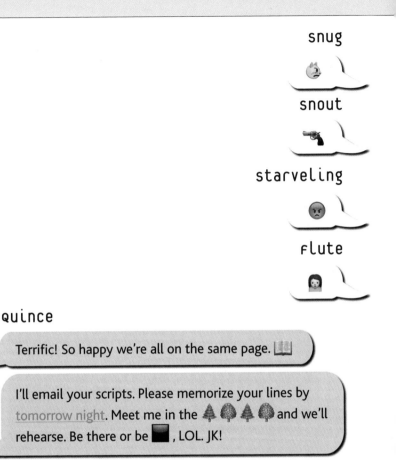

Send

Act 2

Send

[Scene 1]

oberon

Soooo . . . wanna explain what's going on? 

That new from India should be one of my knights, not hanging out with you.

Titania

I can't even with you. 

oberon

Excuse me. As my wife, you're supposed to, IDK, listen to me!

Titania

You're pulling the MARRIAGE card? OK, then! Maybe you'd like to explain why you're sooo in with Hippolyta. You keep leaving our to woo her, and everyone knows it.

oberon

HDU. Also, you're such a hypocrite. As if you aren't completely into Theseus. Psh. You've sabotaged all his relationships because of it.

Send

Titania

Liiiiiies!

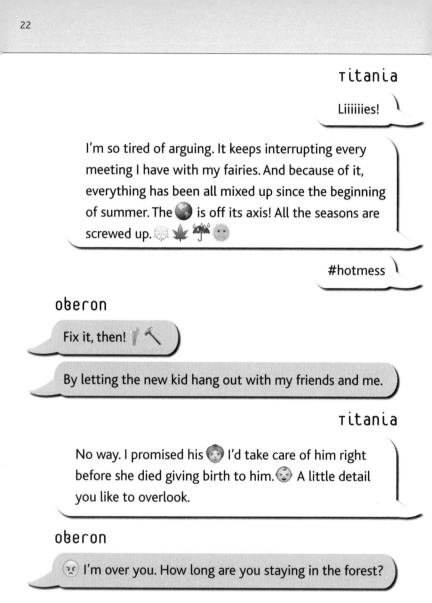

I'm so tired of arguing. It keeps interrupting every meeting I have with my fairies. And because of it, everything has been all mixed up since the beginning of summer. The 🌎 is off its axis! All the seasons are screwed up. ❄️🍁☔🌞

#hotmess

oberon

Fix it, then! 🔧🔨

By letting the new kid hang out with my friends and me.

Titania

No way. I promised his 👩 I'd take care of him right before she died giving birth to him. 👶 A little detail you like to overlook.

oberon

😠 I'm over you. How long are you staying in the forest?

Send

Titania

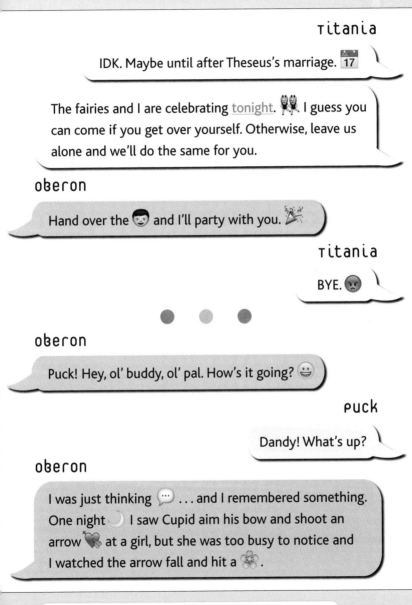

IDK. Maybe until after Theseus's marriage. 17

The fairies and I are celebrating tonight. I guess you can come if you get over yourself. Otherwise, leave us alone and we'll do the same for you.

oberon

Hand over the and I'll party with you.

Titania

BYE.

oberon

Puck! Hey, ol' buddy, ol' pal. How's it going?

puck

Dandy! What's up?

oberon

I was just thinking . . . and I remembered something. One night I saw Cupid aim his bow and shoot an arrow at a girl, but she was too busy to notice and I watched the arrow fall and hit a .

Send

oberon

I kinda sorta maybe definitely need that 🌸 now. I showed it to you once. Remember?

puck

Okeydoke, but why?

oberon

Because, tbh, if you rub it onto someone's 👀 while they're 😴, then when they wake up, they'll fall in 😍 with the first person they see.

Bring it to me quickly, please.

puck

Aye-aye, captain. 

BACK **OBERON** +

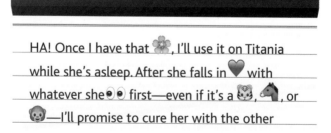

HA! Once I have that 🌸, I'll use it on Titania while she's asleep. After she falls in ❤ with whatever she 👀 first—even if it's a 🐯, 🐴, or 🐵—I'll promise to cure her with the other

Send

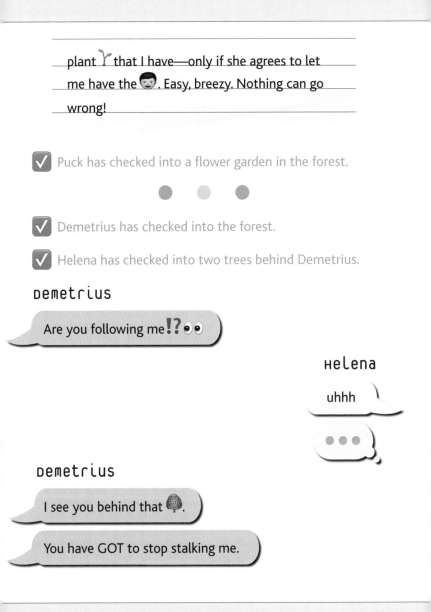

plant 🌱 that I have—only if she agrees to let me have the 👦. Easy, breezy. Nothing can go wrong!

✅ Puck has checked into a flower garden in the forest.

● ● ●

✅ Demetrius has checked into the forest.

✅ Helena has checked into two trees behind Demetrius.

Demetrius

Are you following me⁉️👀

Helena

uhhh

•••

Demetrius

I see you behind that 🌳.

You have GOT to stop stalking me.

Send

Helena

nmf. i'm so crazy about u. u hold this power over me!

i can't let go until u let go of me.

Demetrius

WTF. 😡 I tell you constantly that I. Don't. Love. You. Never have, never will. Is that #closure enough?

Helena

😨 💔 if it wasn't for me, u wouldn't even know about hermia and lysander running away. so yw.

Demetrius

And I've been going in 🌀 🌀 trying to find them. Were you really lying? Was this a trick to be alone with me?

Helena

no, i swear! i'm like ur little 🐶. i'm always going to follow u around. it's kinda cute, y/y? 🐾

Demetrius

Ugh, you make me 😷.

You shouldn't be here, you know, all alone in the woods.

Send

Helena

i'm not alone if ur here. 

Demetrius

I wish a wild 🐗 would eat you. You're so annoying!

Helena

ur crueler than any 🐗, so it's nbd.

Demetrius

OMG. That's it. I'm leaving. 🏃

And you better not follow me!

Helena

this is so messed up. u should be the one chasing me, u know! 😞 😭

• • •

Oberon

Hey, buddy! Did you get the 🌸 ?

Puck

Yep! I'll bring it over in a sec.

Send

oberon

Awesome! I want you to keep some of it as well.

I'm going to find Titania. But with your part, I need you to do me a favor.

I overheard a couple fighting in the forest just now. Can you perform a little switcheroo? Find the man from Athens, and make sure you rub a huge amount of the on his . He'll be chasing her for once, hehehe. TTYL!

[Scene 2]

Titania

Woo-hoo! Can't wait to and celebrate all night long! Twist, twirl, shake it off . . . and then my fairies will sing me to sleep. I LOVE love! Congrats, T+H!

Theseus, Hippolyta, and 5 others like this. REPLY

Hippolyta: Thx, sweetie! xoxo

Oberon has checked into Titania's chambers.

Send

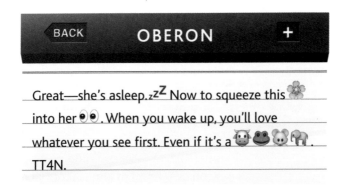

BACK **OBERON** +

Great—she's asleep. zzZ Now to squeeze this into her . When you wake up, you'll love whatever you see first. Even if it's a . TT4N.

● ● ●

☑ Lysander and Hermia have checked into a part of the forest they swear they've seen before.

☑ Lysander has checked into a grassy knoll.

☑ Hermia has checked into a cozy bush a few trees away from Lysander.

Lysander

Hey, what are you doing all the way over there?

IDK. Maybe we shouldn't sleep so close together.

Lysander

Sorry! I wasn't trying to get fresh with you—promise.

Send

Lysander

I just think it would be nice to finally be close to each other. The whole night. 🌟🌙

Two 🖤🖤, one sweet spot.

Hermia

Ooh, you flirt. I'm almost convinced.

But it's better this way. 😘 We have to be good until we're married. 💍

Lysander

Amen.  Sweet dreams!

😍 Lysander

Can't find my way out of Athens, but at least I get to sleep next to my bae. —feeling lost 🌀

 REPLY

● ● ●

✅ Puck has checked into the forest.

Send

BACK **PUCK** +

I've been running around this forest all day and I haven't seen anyone from Athens! I'm exhausted. Aha! A couple sleeping. So this must be the guy who doesn't love this girl. I know what to do. Hope this makes you fall in love with her so hard that you'll never sleep again.

Demetrius has checked into a different part of the forest.

Helena

can u plz slow down?? i can't keep up w/u.

Helena has checked into four trees behind Demetrius.

Demetrius

You're more attached to me than my own shadow! Get a clue. I'm trying to lose you.

Send

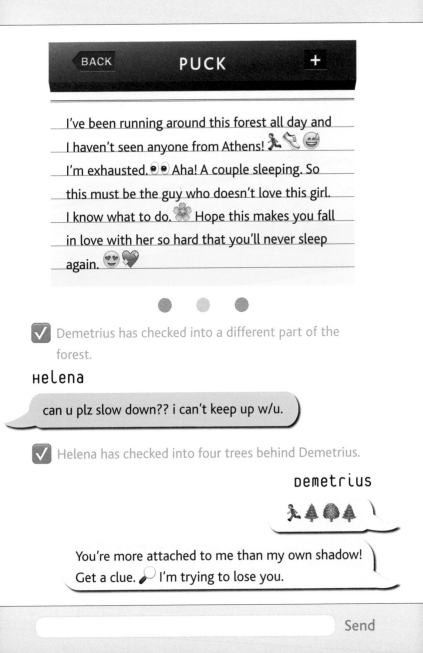

Helena

fine. leave me here in the dark. idc n-e-more. 

Demetrius

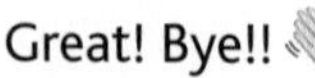
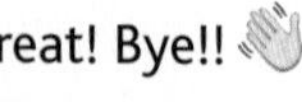

Great! Bye!!

 Helena

life is a bottomless pit. i'll never be good enuf for him—feeling bummed.

 Helena and two others like this. REPLY

 Helena has checked into the grassy brush.

Helena

lysander, is that u? u awake?

Lysander

YAWN. I was just resting my eyes.

Wait.

Send

Helena, is that you over there? 

How have I never noticed before? You're so beautiful! You're as bright as the today!

Is Demetrius with you? I could kill him for the way he treats you!

Helena

y? it doesn't matter. he luvs hermia, but she luvs u.

u don't have n-e-thing to worry about. ur lucky. be happy w/hermia.

Lysander

Happy with Hermia!? Yeah right.

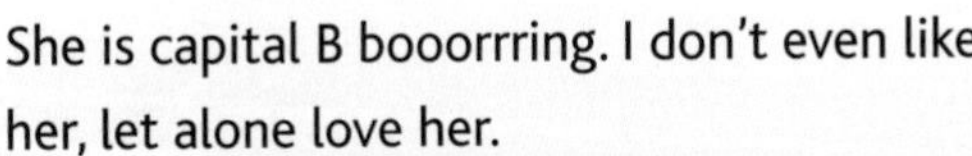

She is capital B booorrring. I don't even like her, let alone love her.

In fact, I love YOU, Helena! 

Helena

stop! stahp!!!

Send

Helena

y does everyone think it's ok to make fun of me and treat me so badly?

i can't handle this abuse. l8r.

Wait! I mean it. You have my heart! 

Look, I'm leaving Hermia behind right now. She's too sweet anyway. She gives me a stomachache.

Hasta la vista, Hermia.

Hermia

Mmm. I slept so peacefully, sweetie.

Lys? You there?

WTF. WHERE ARE YOU? LYS? HELLO???

You can't hide forever. I'll find you! Or die trying!

Send

Act 3

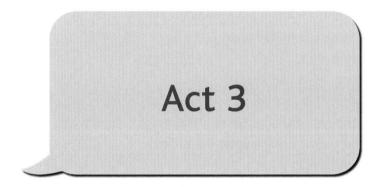

Send

[Scene 1]

Chat Server

Quince: Everyone ready?

Quince: The forest is the perfect place to rehearse. 🎭 There's so much space.

Bottom: Uh, Quince?

Quince: What's up, B?

Bottom: There are parts of this play that will never work. 😟

Bottom: At one point, Pyramus tries to kill himself with a 🔪. That's gonna upset the audience.

Snout: 😨

Starveling: Mabes we should leave out all the death scenes.

Bottom: Well, that's boring. 💡 I've got an idea.

Bottom: Someone should write a prologue that's all "Yeah, there are 🔪🔪 in this play, but no one is ACTUALLY hurt. Pyramus isn't really 💀, and I'm only PRETENDING to be Pyramus." That'll clear things up!

Quince: 👍 We can write that. 📝

Snout: What about Snug as the 🐯? Isn't that gonna scare people too?

Snug: OK, you keep using the tiger for the lion.

Bottom: I see your point, Snout 🐽. Nothing scarier than a wild 🐯.

Snout: So we'll need two prologues.

Send

Bottom: And he should also say something at the beginning like, "No worries! I'm not a real 🐯. It's me—Snug!" 😀

Quince: Awesome! That's settled. But what are we going to do about the lighting?

Quince: Pyramus and Thisbe meet by 🌙💡.

Snout: Hmm, is it going to be a clear night when we perform? 🌃

Bottom: Let's look up the five-day forecast.

Quince: I'm on it.

Tues.	Wed.	Thurs.	Fri.	Sat.
☀🌙	☀🌙	☀🌙	☀🌙	☀🌙

Chat Server

Quince: Excellent! We're in the clear.

Bottom: Perf. So we'll leave a window open so some light can shine in. ✨

Quince: K, but there's still one other thing. There's supposed to be a big wall. In the play, Pyramus and Thisbe talk through a ⚫ in a wall.

Snout: We'll never be able to bring a WALL in. Right, B?

Send

Bottom: No, but someone can act like a wall! We'll just need to cover him in something big 'n' bulky and have him hold out his like this.

Quince: Sounds great! Can we start rehearsing now?

Bottom:

Snug:

Snout:

Starveling:

Flute:

Bottom, Quince, Flute, Snug, Snout, and Starveling have checked into the forest.

quince

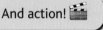

OK, "Pyramus," you're up first. After you've said your lines, go hide in that .

Everyone else, take your places.

And action!

Puck

I never knew the forest could be so fun! Randomly stumbled upon a play rehearsal. It's hilariously bad! Gonna secretly record this and type it up for you guys later—feeling mischievous.

Theseus, Hippolyta, and 7 others like this. REPLY

Puck

OK, here it is!! I kept my observations in too. Enjoy!

REPLY

This Better Be a Dress Rehearsal

Quince: *Ahem, Bottom, you missed your cue. You're Pyramus.*

Bottom: *Oh, right.*

Bottom: *I'll take it from: "Thisbe, come here, with odious smells."*

Quince: *No, no. Not odious. ODORS.*

Bottom: *Oops, my b.*

Bottom: *with odors and smells as sweet as your breath. What's that I hear? A voice? BRB.*

Send

 Puck

K, Bottom is the worst Pyramus I've ever seen. Wait. I have a brilliant idea. I'm going to turn him into something else . . . hehehe.

 REPLY

— This Better Be a Dress Rehearsal —

Flute: *My turn?*

Quince: *Yes! As Thisbe, you're supposed to show that you understand what Pyramus is doing.*

Flute: *Pyramus, you are the best. I'll meet you at Ninny's grave!*

Quince: *NINUS'S grave. Ugh, amateurs.*

Quince: *Bottom, you missed your cue again. You're supposed to come back.*

Bottom: *HERE I AM!*

Send

Quince: *Ahhh! Everyone, run! It's a monster!*

Bottom: *Hello? Where are you?*

 Puck

Don't worry, guys. I'm sticking with Bottom! I won't abandon him. I'll follow him wherever he goes, but I'll stay out of sight.

REPLY

— This Better Be a Dress Rehearsal —

Bottom: *Very funny, guys. Ha-ha. You can come back.*

✅ Snout and Quince have checked into the bushes near the rehearsal grounds.

— This Better Be a Dress Rehearsal —

Snout: *B, you've changed! What's on your head?*

Bottom: *Rude! This is the face I was born with.*  *Why are you acting like a fool?*

Send

Snout: *Excuse me* ⁉️ *You're freaking me out. See ya.* ✌️

Quince: *Gotta agree, Bottom. Enough fooling around. I expect you to be professional the next time we rehearse.*

Bottom: *Why are you guys messing with me? I'm not falling for it! I'm just gonna keep singing without a care. AWAY from you punks.* 🎵🎶

 Titania

Oberon thinks I'm in love with Theseus? Yeah, right. I'll show him. #neverhurtstolook

 REPLY

Send

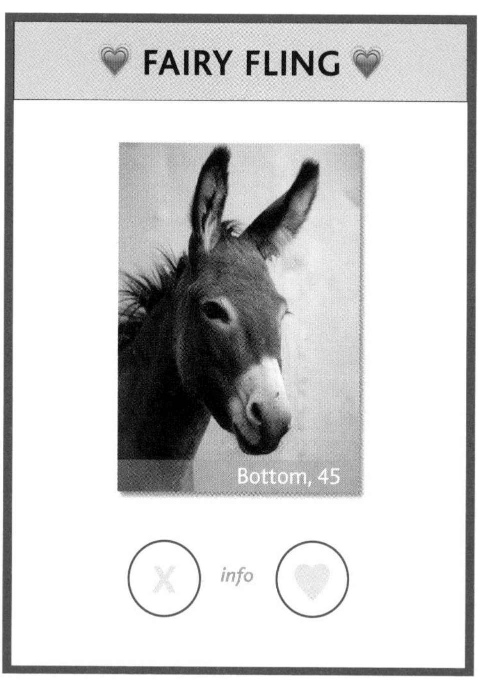
FAIRY FLING
Bottom, 45
X
info

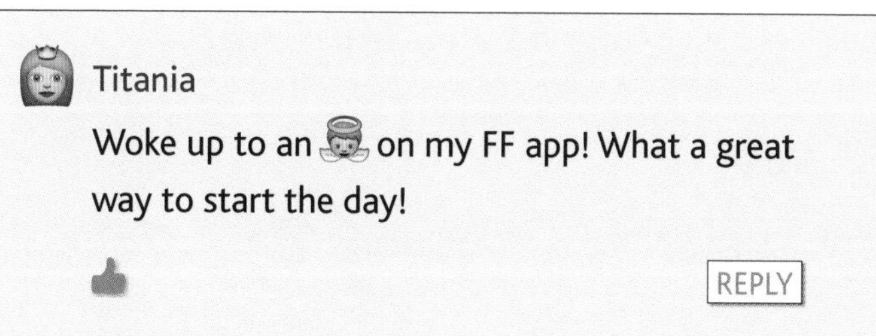
Titania
Woke up to an on my FF app! What a great way to start the day!
REPLY

Send

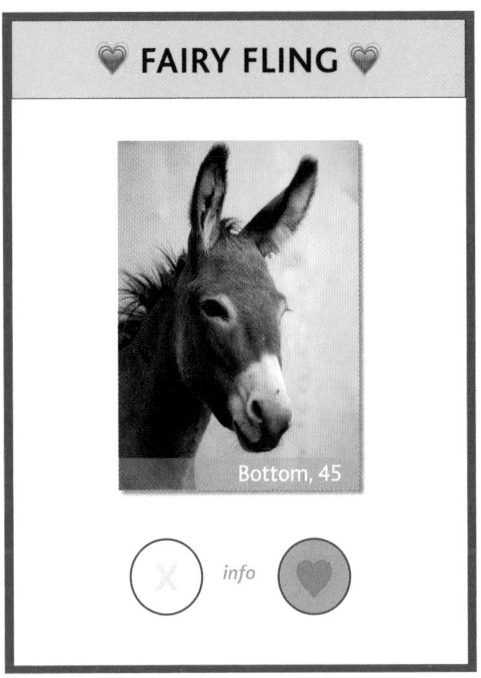

FAIRY FLING MESSAGE

Titania

Who are you? You're so handsome! 😄

I know this will sound cuh-razy, but . . . I think I believe in love at first sight. 

Send

Bottom

Who, me? Uh, I'm not sure there's any reason to be in 🖤 with me. Don't you think you're moving a little fast?

Then again, nothing makes a whole lotta sense when it comes to love.

Titania

Beautiful AND smart. Cha-ching! 💰

Bottom

If I'm so smart, why can't I figure out this app?

Titania

It finds people based on their location. 📍 We must be close! Are you in the 🌳🌲🌳?

Bottom

Yes, and I don't know how to get out of it!

Titania

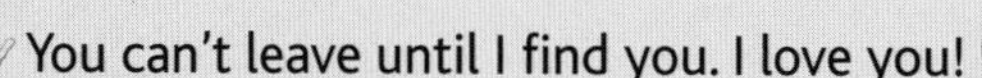

✋ You can't leave until I find you. I love you! 😘

Send

Titania

My name's Titania. I'm the fairy in charge of summer. ☼ If you come with me, I'll give you everything you want! 😀 Want to live forever? NP! And the other fairies will serve you. Lemme reach out to them.

• • •

Group text: Titania, Peaseblossom, Cobweb, Moth, Mustardseed, Bottom

Titania

Heya!

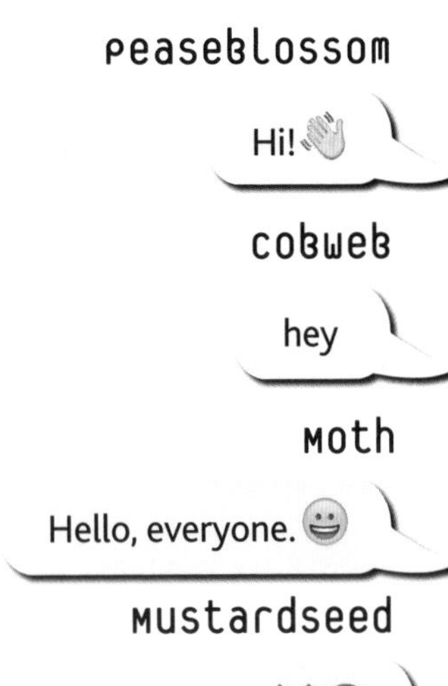

Send

Titania

HUGE favor! Please take care of this handsome man, Bottom.

We're in love, and he should be treated like royalty. 

Thanks so much! 😘 Love you!

peaseblossom

Hi, Bottom! 

cobweb

hey

Moth

Hello, new boy. 

Mustardseed

IT'S SO NICE TO MEET YOU!!! ❌⭕

Send

Bottom

Nice to meet all of you. I hope we get to know each other a little better.

Titania

You will! Everyone, take good care of my love.💑TTYS!

[Scene 2]

Oberon

Puck! Whattya been ⬆️ to?

Puck

Umm, a lot! Lemme break it down for ya.

Titania is in love with a 🐴! While she was sleeping, a bunch of "actors" came by to rehearse a play for Theseus's wedding. 🎭The wackiest one, Bottom, went off alone to wait for his next cue . . . and then I stuck a donkey's head on him! Just for kicks.

His friends were so terrified that they ran away. 😱 But theeeen, Titania woke up, saw him on Fairy Fling, and immediately fell in love. LOL.

Send

oberon

This. Is. AWESOME! 😄

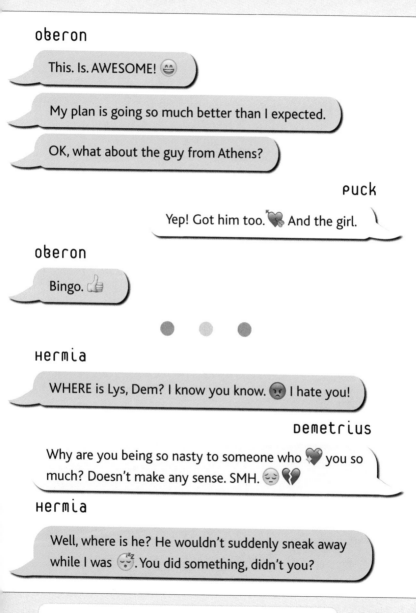

My plan is going so much better than I expected.

OK, what about the guy from Athens?

puck

Yep! Got him too. 💘 And the girl.

oberon

Bingo. 👍

● ● ●

Hermia

WHERE is Lys, Dem? I know you know. 😡 I hate you!

Demetrius

Why are you being so nasty to someone who 💖 you so much? Doesn't make any sense. SMH. 😔💔

Hermia

Well, where is he? He wouldn't suddenly sneak away while I was 😴. You did something, didn't you?

Send

Demetrius

No! HDU?

Hermia

If you're innocent, then help me find him. 🔎

Demetrius

Absolutely not. I'd rather feed him to the 🐶🐶🐶.

Hermia

You're the 🐶. Just tell the truth for once. Did you hurt him?

Demetrius

NO. You're getting all 😠 for no reason.

Hermia

Tell me he's 👌, then.

Demetrius

If I do, will that get me off the hook? 🎣

Send

Hermia

Urgh. It means you'll never see me again, even if he's alive. I can't stand you. BYE.

Demetrius

Whatever. I'm taking a nap. zzZ

oberon

Ugh. WHAT THE PUCK!

You gave the potion to the wrong people!

Puck

Are you suuure? Ruh-roh. 

Welp, must be fate, then!

oberon

Go find Helena right now and bring her here so I can fix your mistake.

I'll put the back on Demetrius's eyes, so when he wakes up again and sees her, it'll all be fixed.

Send

puck

OK! I'll be as fast as an arrow shot from a bow. 
Get it? See ya!

I'm baaack! Told you I'd be fast. 

Helena is nearby and so is the guy I confused for the other one. He's begging her to love him—it's hilarious!  Can we take a break and watch them? Srsly, it's so good.

oberon

No, you idiot. We don't want Demetrius to wake up yet.

puck

But then two guys will be after the same girl. That's even funnier!

oberon

You need help.

 Lysander and Helena have checked into another part of the forest one mile away from the last part they were in.

Send

Lysander

Whyyy won't you talk to me? Do you think I'm joking when I say I love you? I've cried over you. Hello! That should prove I'm serious.

Helena

ur such a liar! u've said the same stuff to hermia.

u can't feel that way about BOTH of us. 

Lysander

I wasn't in the right frame of mind before.

Demetrius has checked into the forest on Lysander and Helena's trail.

Demetrius

Helena? Is that you? You're stunning! Gorgeous! Absolutely the most beautiful thing I've ever seen!

Helena

demetrius? o, not this again. i'm of everyone ganging up on me!

Send

Helena

ugh, u know what? forget it. if ur both going to torture me, u might as well do it together. 👬

Helena has added Demetrius to the group text.

Helena

i'm not some running joke for u guys to laugh at. 😠

Lysander

That's right, you're not!

Demetrius, I know you've loved Hermia all along. Listen, you can have her! I want to be with Helena. Then we'll all be happy. 👫 👫

Demetrius

No thx. Hermia's all yours. I was only into her for a sec. It's Helena I want to ❤️ forever.

Lysander

He's lying, Helena.

Helena

i'm going to block both of ur numbers! i h8 this. 😒

Demetrius

I'm not lying! I'll prove it. Hold on.

Chat Server: MIDSUMMER MISSED CONNECTIONS

Oberon has joined the chat room

Demetrius, Hermia, Lysander, and Helena have joined the chat room

Demetrius: Hermia, you there?

Hermia: Lys, you're here?? Why did you leave me!?

Lysander: I needed to be with someone else.

Hermia: Who!?

Lysander: Helena, duh. She's everything I've ever wanted. And you're not, so bye.

Hermia: 

Helena: o so SHE'S in on this too?

Helena: i can't believe ur all ganging up on me!

Helena: i thought u were my friend, herm.

Hermia: IDK what you're talking about.

Helena: didn't u send lysander after me? and now u have demetrius pretending to be in with me even though he was straight up calling me a fugly just the other day.

Send

Helena: i'm outta here. have a great laugh at my expense. i'm used to it by now.

Lysander: No, stay! Beautiful Helena, don't go.

Lysander: Are you a ? Because every time I look at you, I .

Lysander:

Hermia: Stop the joke, Lys. She's obvi upset.

Demetrius: Srsly, dude. Enough.

Demetrius: Besides, I love her way more than you do.

Lysander: I'll fight you for her, Demetrius!

Demetrius: YOU'RE ON!

Hermia: Boys, stop!

Lysander: Go AWAY, Hermia. Quit chasing me like a and move on. #purrmanently

Hermia: What happened to my sweet Lys? IDGI.

Lysander: Go away. Shoo.

Hermia: You don't mean that.

Helena: of course he doesn't & neither do u!

Demetrius: Hi, hello. We're supposed to be fighting!

Hermia: Look what you've done, Helena. You . IDK how you did it, but you stole Lys's somehow.

Hermia: I should fight you too!

Send

Helena: everyone leave me alone.

Helena: i'm out of here. tty NEVER, tbh.

Hermia: You can't run away without explaining why you're suddenly all 😍 over Lys.

Helena: i'm NOT. the only 👦 i've ever loved is demetrius.

Helena: plz leave me alone, hermia. ur scaring me. 😟

Lysander: Don't worry, Helena. I'll protect you from her.

Demetrius: Can you STFU already? 😠 She doesn't want you.

Lysander: That's it. You and me, right now—we're going to settle this. We'll fight for her. 💪 👊

Demetrius: YEAH, WHAT I'VE BEEN SAYING ALL ALONG.

Demetrius and Lysander have exited the chat room.

Hermia: Way to go, HELL-ena. 🔥

Hermia: Have fun living with your guilty conscience about this whole sitch.

Helena: i can't even rn.

Helena: i'm going to bed. nite. 💤

Hermia: Yeah, well, I was going to bed first!

Hermia: 😴 See? Already asleep.

Helena and Hermia have exited the chat room.

● ● ●

Send

oberon

Do you have ANY idea what's going on between all of them?

Do you KNOW what you've done !?

puck

OK, I deserve that. I made a teeny, tiny mistake. But I did exactly what you said! I put the 🌸 on the Athenian guy's 👀. I didn't know there was another guy running around the forest.

And anyway, who cares? This is so entertaining and trippy.

oberon

You have to fix everything before it gets worse. Here's what you do:

Make it so dark that it's like night. 🌙⭐

Send

Imitate Lysander and insult Demetrius. Then switch it up ⬆️⬇️ and pretend to be Demetrius and 🔍 on Lysander. Keep changing directions so they end up getting separated. But make sure they end up near the right 👧. Eventually, they'll be too exhausted and need to 😴. Just like Helena and Hermia.

When they're asleep, crush this 🌸 onto Lysander's eyes and it'll all be good again. 👍

While you're doing that, I need to find Titania and undo THAT spell so she's not in love with a 🐴 anymore.

Got it??

puck

OK! Off I go. 🏃 I'm gonna need new 👟👟 after all this.

● ● ●

555-5555

Hey, loser! I'm ready to fight. 🔪 Where are you?

Send

Lysander

Who is this?

555-5555

Oh, sars. It's Demetrius. My phone battery died so I had to break out my mom's old flip phone. ☎️ #soancient

Lysander

Oh.

K, I'm coming.

from: heyitslys@midsummer.org
To: youvereacheddemetrius@midsummer.org

Come out, come out, wherever you are, you coward!

from: youvereacheddemetrius@midsummer.org
To: heyitslys@midsummer.org

Huh? 😕 I don't recognize this email.

Send

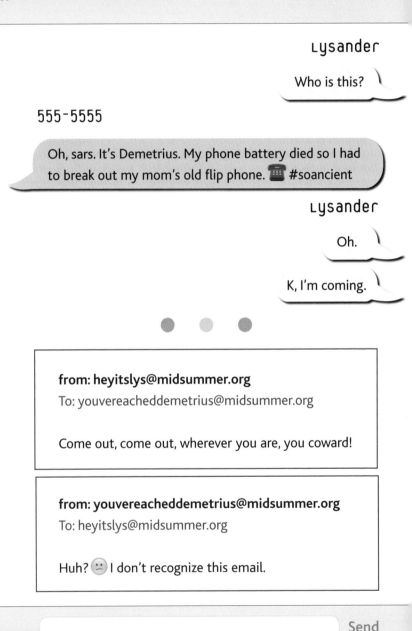

from: heyitslys@midsummer.org
To: youvereacheddemetrius@midsummer.org

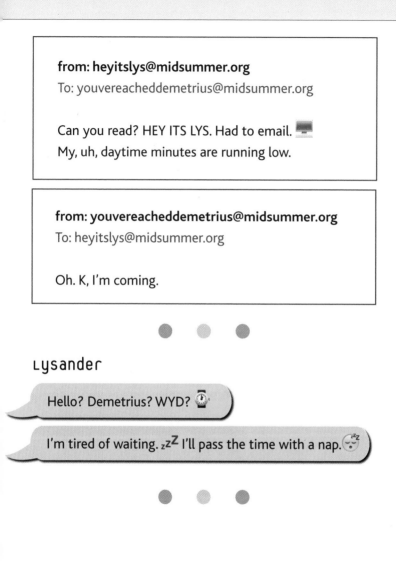

Can you read? HEY ITS LYS. Had to email.
My, uh, daytime minutes are running low.

from: youvereacheddemetrius@midsummer.org
To: heyitslys@midsummer.org

Oh. K, I'm coming.

Lysander

Hello? Demetrius? WYD?

I'm tired of waiting. zzZ I'll pass the time with a nap.

Send

from: youvereacheddemetrius@midsummer.org

To: heyitslys@midsummer.org

[5 minutes ago]

I'm here.

from: youvereacheddemetrius@midsummer.org

To: heyitslys@midsummer.org

[3 minutes ago]

And you're clearly not.

from: youvereacheddemetrius@midsummer.org

To: heyitslys@midsummer.org

[2 minutes ago]

I'm too tired for this. Gonna sleep, but wake me up when you get here! 😴

puck

Everything is all set on my end, O!

Putting the 🌸 onto Lysander's 👀.

Done! He'll wake up and everything will be right again. YW!

Send

Act 4

Send

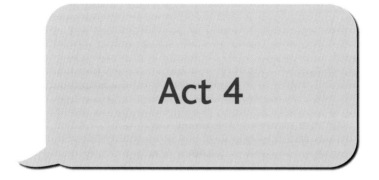

[Scene 1]

oberon

Oh, heyyy, T. How ya been?

Titania

FANTASTIC!

oberon

I was wondering if you gave any more thought to letting me hang out with the new from India?

Titania

Whatever you want! I don't mind! I'm over the happy, O.

G2G! Meeting up with someone. TT4N.

Titania

Bottom, come over and let me pinch those cheeks! Oh, I just love you. I want to kiss you all day.

Send

Bottom

Um, maybe hold up a sec.

Bottom

Hey, Cobweb. You there?

Cobweb

yeah

Bottom

Can you do me a favor?

Cobweb

Bottom

Great! Can you go kill a for me and bring back the ? Thx!

Cobweb

uh. k.

Send

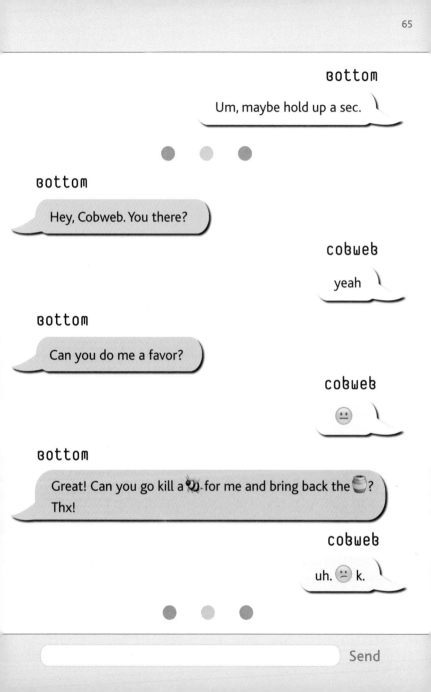

Titania

Want to some , my love?

Or do you want to get something to eat? 

Bottom

Wow, that all sounds great. Really.

But MAN, am I tired. I need to rest these peepers. 

Titania

Absolutely. Go to sleep, sweetie. I'll rest too and ask everyone to give us some privacy.

Oberon

Good news, buddy!

I ran into Titania in the forest, and she's so dumbstruck in with that guy that she agreed to what I wanted right away!

So now we just need to undo the spell for everyone. So it'll all be like a weird dream when they wake up.

Send

I'm going to use the 🌸 on Titania now. Let me know how it goes with the others!

👀 Puck

Here I come, you four! 👫 👫 I've got my portion of the 🌸 and I'm going to set everything straight again. #callmecupid

👍 Oberon likes this. REPLY

● ● ●

oberon

Honey, wake up.

Wakey, wakey, my 👸 .

Titania

O? 😕 I just had the weirdest dream. I was in love with a 🐴!

oberon

Shh, shh, shh. Don't worry. Everything is better now. 

Send

Oberon

Remember, we still have our friends' wedding to celebrate. We should head out.

Titania

OK. Fill me in on the details while we walk. Like how I ended up 😴 on the ground. 🌾

☑ Theseus, Hippolyta, and Egeus have checked into the forest.

Group text: Theseus, Hippolyta, Egeus

Theseus

Whoa! OMG. 😨 Who are these people sleeping on the ground? Come quick!

Hippolyta

do we have to text so much?? i've used up 75% of my monthly data! i don't wanna get charged extra. 😔 💸

Egeus

That's my daughter, Hermia! And Lysander, Demetrius, and Helena. What are they all doing here? 😕

Send

Theseus

Maybe they came here to party a lil bit? 

That reminds me, though. Isn't today the deadline for Hermia's decision? 📅

We've gotta wake 'em up!

Theseus has added Lysander, Demetrius, Helena, and Hermia to the group chat.

Theseus

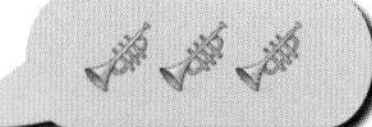

Good morning, lovebirds! 

Lysander

Good morning, Theseus.

Sorry you're seeing me like this. Don't know how we fell asleep out here. 😕

Theseus

Maybe this means you two enemies are finally friends? 

Send

Lysander

The truth is . . . I came here with Hermia. We planned on running away to get married and escape the law.

Egeus

RUNNING AWAY!? Did you that? We need to punish him!

Demetrius

Can I interrupt for a sec?

Hippolyta

no! bc now i've used up ALL my data. next person who talks has to pay my fee.

Demetrius

I'm here because the gorgeous Helena told me Hermia and Lysander were running away. I went after Hermia, and Helena followed me.

I'm not sure why I chased Hermia so much, because I realize now that the only person I love is Helena. I want to be with her!

Send

Theseus

This is fan-TAS-tic! 

You two couples will be married alongside Hippolyta and me. The more, the merrier!

I gotta run. Hippolyta and Egeus, you comin? See you guys tonight at the temple!

Hippolyta

and i'll c u soon, demetrius, so u can pay my bill.

Group text: Demetrius, Hermia, Helena, Lysander

Demetrius

Last night was so weird.

Hermia

Right? My mind feels so fuzzy.

Helena

ditto. and did i hear u right, demetrius? that was almost too weird. like stumbling upon a outta the blue.

Send

Demetrius

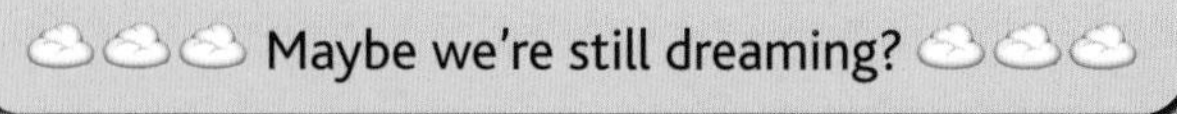

Maybe we're still dreaming?

Lysander

I guess we should listen to Theseus and meet up with him tonight. Maybe things will make sense by then.

 Bottom

I can't BELIEVE the night I had. It was NUTS. 🌀🌀 Wait until Quince and Flute and Snout and the others 👂 about it!

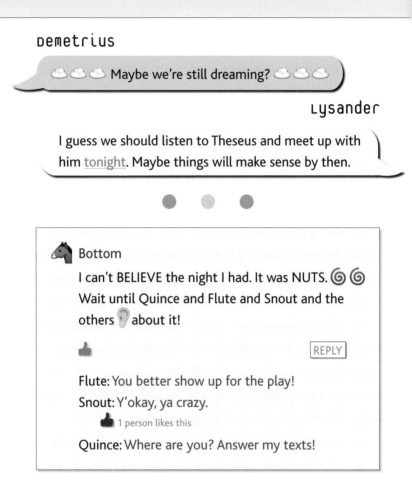 

REPLY

Flute: You better show up for the play!

Snout: Y'okay, ya crazy.

1 person likes this

Quince: Where are you? Answer my texts!

[Scene 2]

Group text: Quince, Starveling, Flute, Snout, Snug, Bottom

Send

quince

Has anyone Bottom yet? He must be . I saw his status update.

starveling

Nada! Do you think he was kidnapped and only just released !?

flute

Maybe he was abducted by .

quince

He better show up or the entire play is ruined. 

snout

Has anyone heard from Snug?

snug

I'm on my way! I'm coming from the .

Theseus and Hippolyta are married. And so are two other couples.

I can't believe we weren't able to put on our play. 

Send

Flute

We couldabin rich! 💰💸 Let's find out what happened to Bottom. I'm texting him again.

You alive, B?

Bottom

Ciao, you guys!

Quince

B! What a RELIEF. 😅 Where have you been?

Bottom

I have SO much to tell you! 😃 But I can't right now.

We have to hurry. We don't have a lot of 🕒. Grab a bunch of new clothes and props. We're putting on this play after all! 🎭

No time to explain. Just hurry. LET'S GO!

Send

Act 5

Send

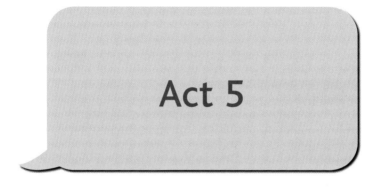

[Scene 1]

Hippolyta

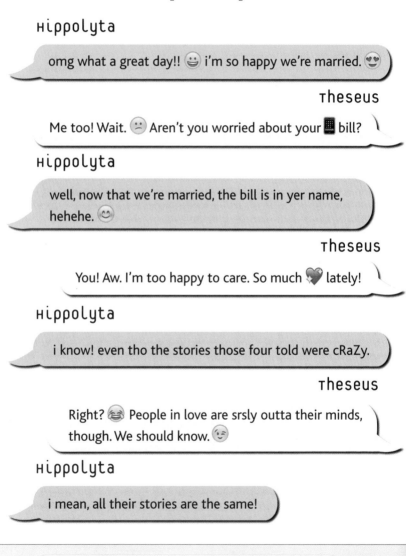

omg what a great day!! 😀 i'm so happy we're married. 😍

Theseus

Me too! Wait. 😕 Aren't you worried about your 📱 bill?

Hippolyta

well, now that we're married, the bill is in yer name, hehehe. 😊

Theseus

You! Aw. I'm too happy to care. So much 💖 lately!

Hippolyta

i know! even tho the stories those four told were cRaZy.

Theseus

Right? 😂 People in love are srsly outta their minds, though. We should know. 😉

Hippolyta

i mean, all their stories are the same!

Send

so even tho it all smells a little , i believe 'em. SHRUG.

Theseus

Samesies. But let's move on. This is a happy day!  

Time for some fun! Lemme text my party planner.

Group text: Theseus, Philostrate, Hippolyta

Theseus

Philostrate, you around?

Philostrate

Holla!

Theseus

What's the 411? What's going on tonight?

Philostrate

I gotchu. There's a whole buncha things.

Send

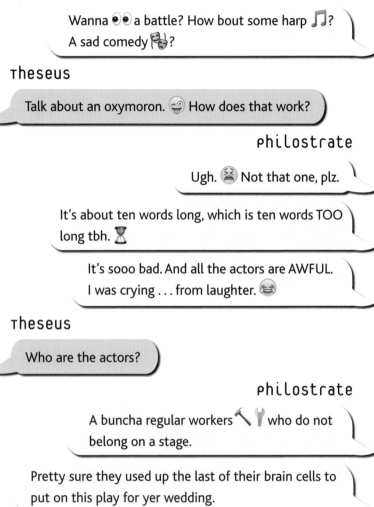

philostrate

Wanna 👀 a battle? How bout some harp 🎵? A sad comedy 🎭?

Theseus

Talk about an oxymoron. 😜 How does that work?

philostrate

Ugh. 😫 Not that one, plz.

It's about ten words long, which is ten words TOO long tbh. ⌛

It's sooo bad. And all the actors are AWFUL. I was crying . . . from laughter. 😂

Theseus

Who are the actors?

philostrate

A buncha regular workers 🔨🔧 who do not belong on a stage.

Pretty sure they used up the last of their brain cells to put on this play for yer wedding.

Send

Theseus

So let's it, then!

Philostrate

OMG are you srs? 

Theseus

Absolutely. Now, go.

Philostrate

All riiight. Didn't think I'd be celebrating yer funeral on the same day as yer wedding, but it's yer choice.

Hippolyta

r u sure about this? he just said they're not good actors.

Theseus

Yeah, c'mon. We're in for a show no matter what! 

Philostrate

We're ready to start with the prologue. All good?

Theseus

#readysetgo

Send

In honor of
Hippolyta and Theseus's wedding,
a full transcript of

"A Very Tragic Comedy About the Horrible Deaths of Pyramus and Thisbe" 🎭🎬

Quince: AHEM. Ladies and gentlemen—if we offend you, it's on purpose. Not even sorry bout it. We're not here to make you 😀. We're here to make you FEEL. 🎭 We hope you're prepared for what you're about to 👀. Please hold all 👏👏 until the end.

Quince: In this play, you'll meet two lovers: Pyramus and a beautiful 👧 named Thisbe. You'll also meet a man portraying the wall the lovers speak through with the best we could come up with 🚪, another man playing the part of the 🌙 because they plan to meet at night, and a man roaring as a 🐯, who scares poor Thisbe, causing her to 🏃 away at night.

Quince: So then basically Thisbe drops her coat, which the 🐯 stains with his bloody mouth, and after

Send

Pyramus finds it, he takes a 🔪 to his 💔, and then Thisbe takes the same 🔪 and kills herself 💀💀, but it's all pretend so don't be 😱!

Quince: Aaand . . . action! 🎬

Snout: I AM A WALL! 🚪

Snout: Well, it's actually me, Snout. And I'm pretending to be a wall. With a ⚫ in the middle so Pyramus and Thisbe can chat through it. Everyone got that??

Theseus: I'm pretty sure actual cement could play this 😞 role better.

Bottom: I am Pyramus!

Bottom: Ohhh, night. 🌃 Oh, night, night, night. It's so sad. Sad, sad, sad. 😔😔😔

Bottom: What a 😔🌃.

Bottom: And where is my Thisbe? Oh, look. A wall! 🚪 It has a ⚫ in it. Let me 👀 if Thisbe is on the other side.

Bottom: Oh, 💩. She's not.

Theseus: Yeesh. That 🚪 should "accidentally" fall on him.

Bottom: Excuse me! It's still my line. Not the 🚪's line.

Bottom: Also, Thisbe, ya missed your cue.

Flute: OH, OOPS. 😱

Flute: Here I am!

Send

Bottom: Thisbe! You're here. 📍

Flute: ILU. ILU. I think. 😍 😘

Bottom: Yeah, ILU too. 💜 And I KNOW it.

Flute: I'll always be faithful to you! 💍

Bottom: Same! Let's 😘 through this nasty 🚪!

Snout: That tickles. 😀

Bottom: Will you meet me at Ninny's grave later tonight? 💀

Flute: Totes! TTYL!

Snout: Welp, I'm done! Wall goes away.

Snout: Oh! Those were my stage directions. OK, bye! 🚪

Theseus: Guess Pyramus and Thisbe should've waited a second longer.

Hippolyta: this is so silly! hehehe. 😂

Theseus: Get ready because I think it's about to get even sillier.

Snug: Hiii. Don't be afraid of me when I roar! I'm not a real 🐯. It's me—Snout! NBD!

Theseus: 😕 *What's with all these disclaimers?*

Demetrius: So far, he's the best actor tbh.

Starveling: And I'm not really a 🌙, but I'm a "🌙" for this play.

Starveling: Think 👨 in the 🌙. I am here to shed 💡.

Hippolyta: booorrring. they should bring back the 🚪 *at this point.*

Send

Helena: hipp, ur so bad! 😉

Lysander: Don't be rude, you guys! 😠

Hermia: Yeah, shh! It's getting good. Uh, I think.

Lysander: Go on, Mr. 🌙.

Starveling: No, that's it. That's all I was gonna say. 😉

Lysander: Oh.

Demetrius: Wow.

Flute: Here I am at Ninny's 💀! WYD, Pyramus?

Snug: 🐯 HEY THERE! 🐯

Snug: I mean. Uh. ROARRR!

Flute: OMG. 😱 No, ty! Bye! 🏃

Helena: awesome roaring, 🐯*!*

Hermia: Nice running, Thisbe! 🏃 *#legday*

Snug: Thisbe dropped her coat. I am going to tear it apart with my teeth now.

Theseus: Way to go, 🐯*! Get it like a* 🐱 *with a* 🐭.

Bottom: Hello, I'm back! Shoo, 🐯.

Snug: G2G. See ya!

Bottom: OMG. What is this? This bloody coat belonged to Thisbe?

Bottom: Oh gawd, that 🐯 killed the love of my life! 💔

Bottom: 😔😭😔😭

Hippolyta: wow, i feel kinda bad for him. 😔

Theseus: I know, me too. Strange.

Bottom: I can't live in this 🌎 anymore!

Send

Bottom: I must take this 🔪 and stab myself in the ❤️. Adieu, cruel world.

Bottom: 💀

Theseus: Should someone get him to a 🏥?

Hippolyta: o no. what's going to happen with thisbe now? 😟

Flute: Wakey, wakey, my love. 😘

Flute: Hello? Pyramus? OMG. What's happened to your 💔? A 🔪?

Flute: I can't believe my 👀.

Flute: If I can't have you in this life, then I'll join you in another.

Flute: 🔪 ❤️ 🔪 💀

Theseus: Wow, that escalated quickly. 📈 Who's going to bury them?

Demetrius: I guess the 🐯. And the 🌙. The 🚪 could help too.

Bottom: Psst. Gotta break character for a sec to let you know that the 🚪 was taken down, so technically it can't help bury us. 💀💀

Bottom: Wanna hear an epilogue ⁉️ 😀

Theseus: Um, no, that's OK.

Theseus: You were all fantastic. Bravo, bravo!

Send

Theseus: But it's ***midnight****, so it's time to .*

Theseus: Don't fret, though. We're gonna keep celebrating for two weeks! G'nite!

Group text: Oberon, Titania, Puck

Oberon

Well, that worked out better than I thought it would. 

Titania

We should and too with all the fairies!

Puck

I that idea! Let's all take a selfie.

Posted! #nofilternecessary #midsummermemories #

Send

 Puck

What a crazy four days it's been! So many mixed-up 🖤 stories. OK, maybe I had a little something to do with that. #trickster But don't be 😠 at me! Maybe the past week has been a ☁️ dream ☁️ all along. Maybe not. It's not up to me to decide—it's up to you. G'nite, everyone! And may you have the sweetest dreams. 😉 😉

👍 21 people like this REPLY

Send

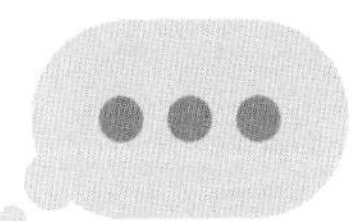

The 411 for Those Not in the Know

411: Information

BRB: Be Right Back

BTW: By The Way

FOMO: Fear Of Missing Out

G2G: Got To Go

H8: Hate

HDU: How Dare You

IDC: I Don't Care

IDGI: I Don't Get It

IDK: I Don't Know

ILU: I Love You

JK: Just Kidding

L8R: Later

NBD: No Big Deal

NMF: Not My Fault

NP: No Problem

OMG: Oh My God

Send

RN: Right Now

SMH: Shaking My Head

STFU: Shut The F*ck Up

TBH: To Be Honest

TL;DR: Too Long; Didn't Read

TT4N: Ta Ta For Now

TTYL: Talk To You Later

TTYS: Talk To You Soon

TY: Thank You

WTF: What The F*ck

WYD: What You Doing

YW: You're Welcome

Y/Y: Yes/Yes

Send

some emotions you might find in this book

- Angry
- Anguished
- Blank (straight)
- Confused
- Dead/Dying
- Devious
- Disappointed
- Embarrassed
- Extremely angry (fuming)
- Extremely funny (crying)
- Extremely sad (crying)
- Flirty
- Friendly (wink, wink)

Send

 Frustrated

 Goofy

 Happy

 Love

 Nervous

 Sad

 Shocked

 Shocked and screaming

 Sick

 Silly

 Sleepy

 Unamused

 Whistle

 Worried

Send

BRETT WRIGHT has a BFA in creative writing and works full-time as a children's book editor in New York City. In college, he studied Shakespearean tragedy, which was sadly lacking in emojis. If he's being honest, he prefers fall 🍂 to summer ☀️. @brettwright

WILLIAM SHAKESPEARE was born in Stratford-upon-Avon in 1564. He was an English poet, playwright, and actor, widely regarded as the greatest writer in the English language and the world's preeminent dramatist. His plays have been translated into every major language and are performed more often than those of any other playwright. 🎭

Send

FOMO?

Read on for a peek at

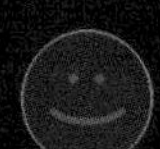

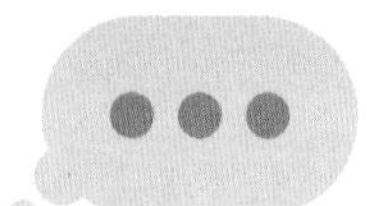

[Scene 3]

 Witch #1

It's 🎉⏰! Where my girls @?

REPLY

Witch #2: Oh, you know, killing 🐷🐷🐷.

Witch #3: U?

Witch #1: Well, I won't bore u w/ the details, but there was a 👫 and a ⛵ and some 🌰s. She didn't want to share, 🐽. Let's just say, it didn't end well for her. LMAO.

Witch #3: I 👂 a drum! Macbeth is almost here. U guys remember the chant?

Witch #1: We weird sisters 👵👵👵. . .

Witch #2: ✋ in ✋, travel all over the 🌍 . . .

Witch #3: 💃💃💃, 3 + 3 + 3 = 9. Yay! The spell is ready. 🔮

Macbeth

Banquo, I'm almost there. This weather is TERRIBLE!! ⚡☔ At least we won! Did you 👀 I'm #Trending?! 📈

Send

Banquo

Congrats!

Hey, can you see those 👵👵👵? WTF! They have longer beards than me.

Witch #1

Hail, Macbeth, Thane of Glamis.

Macbeth

Who are you & how did you get our numbers?! 😠

Witch #2

Hail, Macbeth, Thane of Cawdor.

Banquo

Huh? Macbeth, did u get promoted w/o telling me?

Witch #3

Hail, Macbeth, soon 2 b king. 👑

Banquo

Um, if u can see the future 🔮, can u give me good 📰 2? 😉

Send

witch #1

Banquo, < lesser than Macbeth and greater >.

witch #2

Not as happy 😀, but much happier 😉.

witch #3

You'll have 👑 👶s, but you won't be 👑 yourself.

All hail Macbeth & Banquo! 🙌

Macbeth

Huh? I'm Thane of Glamis already. But IDK anything about Cawdor. Last I heard, that guy was still alive. (And the life of every party! 🍻) And 👑? Well, that's just crazy 🌀🌀! Tell me more . . . ?

Not Delivered

Banquo

Hello??

Not Delivered

Banquo

Hey, Macbeth, my txts to 👵👵👵 aren't goin thru. 😫

Send

Macbeth

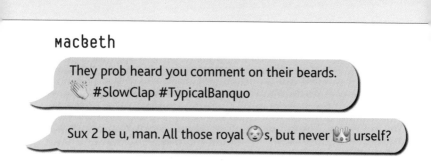

They prob heard you comment on their beards. #SlowClap #TypicalBanquo

Sux 2 be u, man. All those royal s, but never urself?

Banquo

Ha, right. Like ur actually gonna be ! 

Group text: Ross, Angus, Macbeth, Banquo

ROSS

Hey. I know ur still OTW from battle, but just FYI the king is pretty w/ u, Macbeth.

Angus

And . . .

ROSS

He chose u as the new Thane of Cawdor. 

Macbeth

But the old Thane of Cawdor's still alive . . . rite? I don't wear borrowed kilts, if u know what I mean. #ThaneLife

Send

ROSS

Yeah, he's alive, but to the . He admitted to treason and everything. It's all you.

Macbeth

Wow, thx!

Macbeth

Banquo, I'm Thane of Cawdor! Do you think this means your s will be after all?

Banquo

They said u were gonna be remember?! But we should b careful. Maybe it's all a trick.

Macbeth

Yeah, the best trick EVER!

Send

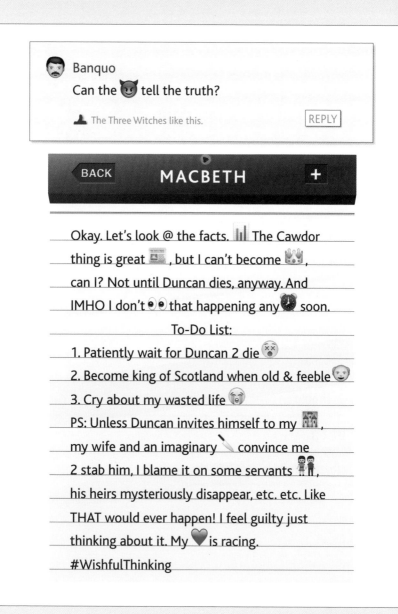

Banquo
Can the tell the truth?

The Three Witches like this.

REPLY

BACK **MACBETH** +

Okay. Let's look @ the facts. The Cawdor thing is great , but I can't become , can I? Not until Duncan dies, anyway. And IMHO I don't that happening any soon.

To-Do List:

1. Patiently wait for Duncan 2 die
2. Become king of Scotland when old & feeble
3. Cry about my wasted life

PS: Unless Duncan invites himself to my , my wife and an imaginary convince me 2 stab him, I blame it on some servants , his heirs mysteriously disappear, etc. etc. Like THAT would ever happen! I feel guilty just thinking about it. My is racing.

#WishfulThinking

Send

BACK **BANQUO** 

Macbeth looks kinda weird rite now. His hair is standing up & I can literally his pounding. Gonna keep my on him. #Creeper

[Scene 4]

Duncan

Hey, son, has the old Thane of Cawdor been "taken care of" yet?

Malcolm

Yep, I've gotten that Cawdor is officially .

Duncan

About ! How'd it go?

Send

Malcolm

He was surprisingly brave. 😯 Prob the most impressive thing he ever did in life was die lol. 😵 🌟 👏 (Too soon??)

Duncan

I still can't believe it. I rly trusted that guy! Never shoulda bought those matching BFF kilts . . .

Group text: Duncan, Macbeth, Banquo

Duncan

Congrats and thx, Macbeth. You've given me more than I could ever repay. 💸

Macbeth

Just having ur 👍 is enough, D. 😀

Duncan

Still, I'll 👀 out for you from now on 💰 💰 💰 & Banquo 2 💰.

Banquo

U gave us the chance to succeed! #Blessed

Send

Duncan

Speaking of succeed—I have an announcement 2 make. Brb.

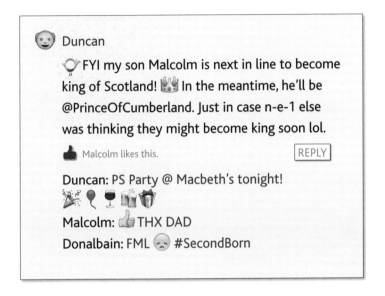

 Duncan

FYI my son Malcolm is next in line to become king of Scotland! In the meantime, he'll be @PrinceOfCumberland. Just in case n-e-1 else was thinking they might become king soon lol.

Malcolm likes this. REPLY

Duncan: PS Party @ Macbeth's tonight!

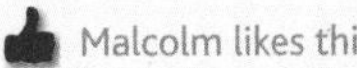

Malcolm:  THX DAD

Donalbain: FML #SecondBorn

 Malcolm

Oh, I just can't wait to be . . . sued for copyright infringement.

 REPLY

Send

BACK
MACBETH
+
UGH! MALCOLM is Prince of Cumberland now? Well, that sux. It's gonna be a lot harder to become . #AlwaysTheThane
Hmm, I gotta keep these s & my black out of the . I need to look !

[Scene 5]

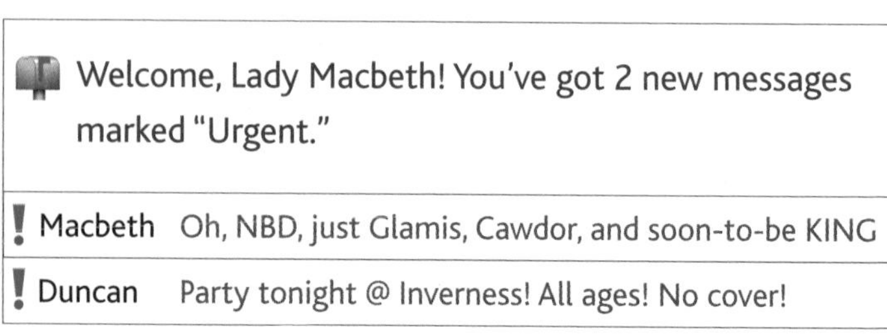
Welcome, Lady Macbeth! You've got 2 new messages marked "Urgent."
! Macbeth Oh, NBD, just Glamis, Cawdor, and soon-to-be KING
! Duncan Party tonight @ Inverness! All ages! No cover!

Send

BACK **LADY MACBETH** +

OMG?! Me, queen of Scotland?? Better start trying on crowns! 👑💁 But Macbeth can be such a 🍼. He's 2 nice to speed up the process, if u know what I mean. 😉 I'll have 2 do some convincing. . . .

Come, 👻👻👻, and change me from a 🚺 to a 🚹. Fill me from head 2 👠 with cruelty. #SorryNotSorry

📥 Lady Macbeth has added 📕 *How to Kill Friends and Influence Peasants* to cart.

Send

But Wait! There's More!

Ghost of Christmas Yet to Come

I see an awesome 🎁 in your future. 🎅

Scrooge

Yeah, great. You people get new OMG  and I get 👻👻👻.

#worstgiftever

Darcy

Speaking of worst things, I just got back from the worst ball EVER. 💏👎

Lizzy

😒 You know I'm on this group text, right? #thisiswhyimsingle

Darcy

😳 Wait, no, you misunderstood. . . .

Jane Austen

Don't worry, Darcy. #hatersgonnadate